D0491511

For Mum and Dad
J.E.

For Aaron
P.I.

PUFFIN BOOKS

Published by the Penguin Group
Penguin Books Ltd, 27 Wrights Lane, London W8 5TZ, England
Penguin Putnam Inc., 375 Hudson Street, New York, New York 10014, USA
Penguin Books Australia Ltd, Ringwood, Victoria, Australia
Penguin Books Canada Ltd, 10 Alcorn Avenue, Toronto, Ontario, Canada M4V 3B2
Penguin Books India (P) Ltd, 11 Community Centre, Panchsheel Park, New Delhi – 110 017, India
Penguin Books (NZ) Ltd, Cnr Rosedale and Airborne Roads, Albany, Auckland, New Zealand
Penguin Books (South Africa) (Pty) Ltd, 5 Watkins Street, Denver Ext 4, Johannesburg 2094, South Africa

Penguin Books Ltd, Registered Offices: Harmondsworth, Middlesex, England

On the World Wide Web at: www.penguin.com

First published by Viking 2000
Published in Puffin Books 2001
1 3 5 7 9 10 8 6 4 2

Text copyright © Jonathan Emmett, 2000
Illustrations copyright © Penny Ives, 2000
All rights reserved

The moral right of the author and illustrator has been asserted

Made and printed in Italy by Printer Trento Srl

British Library Cataloguing in Publication Data
A CIP catalogue record for this book is available from the British Library

ISBN 0–140–56476–4

Fox's New Coat

Jonathan Emmett · Illustrated by Penny Ives

PUFFIN BOOKS

There was a wonderful, new, woollen coat in the clothes' shop window. It had a beautiful pattern that used all the colours of the rainbow, and lots of gold buttons that shone like little suns.

Fox fell in love with it the instant she tried it on.

"It's gorgeous!" she exclaimed. "And just the right size!"

But Squirrel could see that the coat was too long.

"Well," he said slowly, "I would have thought that it was –"

"You would have thought that it was *made for me*!" interrupted Fox, slapping her money on to the counter.

"I know exactly what you mean."

And she swept out of the shop before Squirrel could say another word.

Fox walked home, proudly showing off her new coat.

Her nose was so high in the air, she walked straight into …

… Stork.

"Stork!" said Fox excitedly. "Look at my lovely new coat. Isn't it gorgeous?"

Stork picked himself up and stepped back to admire the coat.

"It is rather splendid," he admitted. Then he noticed something peculiar about the bottom of the coat.

"Gosh," he said, raising an eyebrow, "It looks as if it—"

"It looks as if it was *made for me*, doesn't it?" said Fox, cutting him short. "Well, I must be on my way."

And she rushed off before Stork could say another word.

Fox was on her way home when
she saw ...

… Snake slithering the other way.

"Snake! Snake!" she called. "Come and look at my splendid new coat!"

Snake took a good look at the coat.

"Oh yesssss!" he hissed. "It'sssss ssssssimply ssssspectacular, but wouldn't you sssssay that it'sssss more of a jacket than a coat?"

Snake slithered
around Fox's back.
"Goodnesssss!" he
exclaimed. "It'sssss all –"

"It's almost as if it was *made
for me*! I know!" interrupted Fox.
"Well, I'd love to stop and chat,
but I must get home."
And she hurried off before
Snake could say another word.

Fox was halfway home when she came across …

… Mole digging in her garden.

"Hello, Mole!" she cried. "Do you notice anything *different* about me today?"

"I can't really see you properly!" said Mole, blinking at Fox. "Have you got a new scarf?"

"A new *scarf* !" laughed Fox. "Mole, it's a magnificent new coat. Anyone can see that!"

Mole rubbed her eyes and took another look.

"Oh!" she said hesitantly. "Your coat, Fox, I think it might have been –"

"It might have been *made for me*! I know!" said Fox. "You're not the first to notice!" And off she went before Mole could say another word.

Fox was almost home when she met ...

… Owl taking his afternoon nap.

"Wake up, Owl," she called loudly. "And look at my wonderful new coat. Isn't it the most beautiful thing that you've ever seen?"

Owl opened one eye and inspected Fox, then he opened the other and turned them both slowly down to the ground and back along the path.

"Fox," he said carefully. "Your coat, I think it must have –"

"It must have been *made for me!*"
shrieked Fox in delight. "I know! That's
what everyone's been saying!"

And off she went before Owl could
say another word.

Fox arrived home and
went straight to the mirror
to admire herself.

"IT'S *GONE*!" she
screamed. "My beautiful
new coat has gone!
But how? But where?
But when?"

Just then her friends arrived.
Squirrel was holding a big ball of
multi-coloured wool and a pawful
of shiny gold buttons.

"I'm very sorry, Fox," said Squirrel, "but this is all that is left of your coat.
You caught it in the door on your way out of the shop and it's been unravelling
ever since."

Fox looked so sad that her friends could
not help feeling sorry for her.

"Don't worry!" said Owl brightly. "I've got an idea,"
and he fetched a bagful of knitting needles.
    Then Snake and Stork took Fox's measurements while
everyone else took a piece of the wool and began to
knit … and knit … and knit … until they had made …

... a wonderful,
new, woollen coat!

Fox tried on the coat and this time it was just the right size. She was *almost* speechless with delight.

"It's perfect!" she gasped. "It feels as if –"

"We know," said all her friends at once.

"It feels as if it was *MADE FOR YOU*!"